Simpsons™ COMICS
BEACH BLANKET BONGO

HARPER

NEW YORK • LONDON • TORONTO • SYDNEY

SIMPSONS COMICS BEACH BLANKET BONGO

HarperCollins books may be purchased for educational, business, or sales
promotional use. For information, please e-mail the
Special Markets Department at SPsales@harpercollins.com.

FIRST EDITION

ISBN 978-0-06-123126-1

16 17 18 SCP 10 9 8 7 6 5 4

Publisher: Matt Groening
Creative Director: Bill Morrison
Managing Editor: Terry Delegeane
Director of Operations: Robert Zaugh
Art Director: Nathan Kane
Art Director Special Projects: Serban Cristescu
Production Manager: Christopher Ungar
Legal Guardian: Susan A. Grode

HarperCollins Editors: Hope Innelli, Jeremy Cesarec

Manufactured in China

TABLE OF CONTENTS

SPLOOSH!

AAAH!

HA! HA! HA! HA! HA! HA! HA! HA! HA! HA!

WHOA! SORRY FOR THE *SPLASHAGE*, LITTLE DUDETTE! DIDN'T SEE YOU THERE!

≣SIGH≣

HEY, BART!

YO, BART!

SMEK!

HI, BART!

SMACK!

IT'S MY *FIRST DAY*. WHO'S THIS BART KID?

OH, *EVERYONE* KNOWS BART. HE'S THE *IMPISH TERROR OF TEACHERS EVERYWHERE*.

AND I'M LISA. I'M ON *THE HONOR ROLL, THE YEARBOOK COMMITTEE*, AND--

SHE'S *BART'S SISTER*.

IT MUST BE *GREAT* HAVING SUCH A *COOL* BROTHER!

YEAH... GREAT.

ELSEWHERE...

YAAAH!

SPLOOSH!

HA! HA! HA! HA!

OH, HEY, SORRY ABOUT THAT *PRISONER #203459*. I WAS JUST TESTING THE *RIOT HOSE*. DIDN'T SEE YOU THERE.

꞊SIGH꞊

HI, BOB!

HEY, BOB!

YO, BOB!

I'M *NEW*. WHO'S THAT?

DUDE, THAT'S *HOMICIDAL GENIUS*, SIDESHOW BOB.

I'M A HOMICIDAL GENIUS, TOO. I ALMOST *FLOODED* THE ENTIRE TOWN ONCE!

BOB'S HIS BROTHER.

WOW! IT'S LIKE YOU'RE TITO JACKSON.

YES, ALWAYS A TITO, NEVER A MICHAEL...

...OR EVEN ꞊SHUDDER꞊ A LATOYA.

BOB, IT'S TIME FOR YOUR *MONTHLY* PAROLE HEARING. I HOPE YOU DON'T HAVE ANY *BRILLIANT EVIL SCHEMES* IN PLACE!

OH, HEAVEN FORBID, DEAR JAILKEEPER.

EXCUSE ME. WHAT ABOUT *MY* PAROLE HEARING? WHEN DO *I* GET ONE?

AND YOU ARE?

CECIL TERWILLIGER.

CECIL...CECIL... NOPE, LOOKS LIKE WE NEVER GOT AROUND TO *PROCESSING* YOU.

WHAT?

WELL, IT WAS A *BUSY DAY*. WE WERE BOOKING THAT *NOTORIOUS CRIMINAL MASTERMIND,* SIDESHOW BOB.

WHAT DOES THIS MEAN?

YOU'RE *FREE* TO GO, I GUESS. OH, AND SINCE YOU WEREN'T A PRISONER YOU *OWE* US A YEAR'S *RENT*.

SLAM!

SOON...

WHAT TO DO NOW? WHAT'S MY *NEXT STEP*?

VILLAIN MONTHLY magazine

AHA!

CLASSIFIED HIDEOUTS FOR RENT

KNOCK!

209

KNOCK!

BUT YOU CAN'T *EVICT* ME! I'VE ALMOST *TAKEN OVER THE WORLD*!

BUT...

LIKE YOU'VE *ALMOST* PAID THE RENT THE LAST THREE MONTHS?

TAKE A WALK, DR. COLOSSUS!

I'M HERE ABOUT THE *FURNISHED LAIR*?

¡SOB!¿

YOU GOT FIRST AND LAST MONTH'S RENT?

I HAVE A *MONEY ORDER* RIGHT HERE.

THAT THERE MONITOR THING HAS A *SATELLITE FEED* THAT CAN SEE INTO ANY HOME IN SPRINGFIELD. THE *LASER* IS *FULLY-CHARGED* AND THE *TORTURE VAT* CAN BE FILLED WITH LAVA OR THE SUBSTANCE OF YOUR CHOICE. NO PETS AND NO GIRLS AFTER 11 PM!

¡GASP!¿

AND AFTER I PLAYED THE DIMINISHED F SHARP MY MUSIC TEACHER, MR. LARGO, SAID HE'D NEVER HEARD *THE BLUES* PERFORMED LIKE THAT WITHOUT THE BENEFIT OF *YEARS OF HARD DRINKING.*

MOM, DAD! YOU'RE *NOT LISTENING* TO ME!

WHAT? OH, SORRY, HONEY. WE THOUGHT *BART* WAS GOING TO SAY SOMETHING.

SOMETHING ABOUT HAVING PRINCIPAL SKINNER'S MOM *ARRESTED* BY *THE UNITED NATIONS* FOR *CRIMES AGAINST HUMANITY?*

SHE WAS CLEARED OF ALL CHARGES EVEN-TUALLY. AND SHE GOT A TRIP TO GENEVA.

BUT YOU'RE RIGHT. I'M SORRY. I *LEARNED MY LESSON,* AND I'LL *NEVER* DO IT AGAIN. I'LL *APOLOGIZE* TO HER TOMORROW.

THAT'S BETTER!

YOU KNOW WHAT GOES GREAT WITH AN APOLOGY? *CAKE!*

I WONDER WHAT'S *WRONG* WITH LISA? SHE *STORMED OFF* EARLIER THAN *USUAL* TONIGHT.

AAARGH!

CAN'T TALK! EATING *APOLOGY FROSTING!*

THE NEXT WEEK...

BARK! BARK!

THUD!

MARGE! THE MAIL'S HERE.

SO PICK IT UP.

AAAW! BUT THERE'S *BENDING* INVOLVED.

BUZZ COLA

BILL...BILL... DEATH THREAT ...BILL.

A *DEATH THREAT?* NOT *AGAIN*. IT MUST MEAN MY ARCH ENEMY SIDESHOW BOB IS--

IT'S FOR *LISA*.

WHAT? LET *ME* SEE THAT.

IT *IS* FOR YOU.

REALLY? WHO WOULD SEND *ME* A DEATH THREAT?

LISA SIMPSON, YOUR END IS-NEAR.

BEST REGARDS YOUR MORTAL ENEMY.

EXACTLY! IT MAKES NO SENSE. IT MUST BE FOR ME! GIMME!

BART, LET GO!

IF YOU TWO CAN'T *SHARE,* THEN *NOBODY* GETS THE DEATH THREAT!

MOM!

MOM!

I'M CALLING THE *POLICE* RIGHT NOW.

THIS IS SO TOTALLY A *MISTAKE!*

NO, SIDESHOW BOB IS STILL *LOCKED UP.* I CAN SEE HIM RIGHT NOW WATCHING A PRISON PRODUCTION OF "LES MISERABLES."

OH, PLEASE, ANDREW LLOYD WEBBER MUST BE *SPINNING IN HIS GRAVE.*

HE'S *NOT DEAD,* AND *HE DIDN'T WRITE* "LES MIS."

YES, BUT THAT *PLEASANT THOUGHT* KEEPS MY MIND OFF THIS *DREADFUL RENDITION* OF "MASTER OF THE HOUSE."

BOB'S STILL IN JAIL, HOMER. BUT TO BE SAFE, I WANT YOU TO DRIVE THE KIDS TO SCHOOL.

GOTCHA!

AARGH! HOMER WE'RE *TOO BIG* FOR THESE *BABY SAFETY SEATS.*

I CAN'T *FEEL* MY LEGS.

LISTEN, YOUR MOM WANTED ME TO GET YOU TO SCHOOL *SAFELY,* AND THAT'S HOW YOU'RE GONNA GET THERE!

SHOULDN'T YOU BE WATCHING THE ROAD?

YES. YES, I SHOULD.

SO YOU'RE OKAY WALKING THE REST OF THE WAY, AND $5 EACH MEANS YOUR MOM NEVER HEARS ABOUT THIS?

YES.

HAVE A GOOD DAY AT SCHOOL!

MR. LARGO, WHAT ARE YOU DOING OUT HERE?

MUSIC CLASS HAS BEEN *ELIMINATED* DUE TO THE LATEST ROUND OF *BUDGET CUTS.* I'M TRYING TO MAKE RENT.

AND MATH? HISTORY? SCIENCE? ARE *THEY* CANCELLED, TOO?

NO.

DAGNABBIT!

BUT THIS CAN'T BE!

IF YOU DON'T HAVE ANY *SPARE CHANGE,* KEEP IT MOVING. I'VE GOT SOME *BUSKING* TO DO.

♪ CHICKITY CHINA ♪ THE CHINESE CHICKEN, ♪ YOU HAVE A DRUM- STICK AND YOUR BRAIN STOPS TICKIN'... ♪

PRINCIPAL SKINNER! WHAT'S THIS ABOUT THE MUSIC DEPARTMENT BEING *CUT?*

OH, HELLO LISA. GLAD YOU BARGED IN.

IT'S ALL PART OF THE NEW *MONEY SAVING PLAN* THE *SCHOOL BOARD* HAS INSTITUTED.

BUT WHAT ABOUT MY SAX?

THANKS FOR REMINDING ME! *YOINK!*

GRAB!

YOINK?

IT NOW FALLS INTO THE SCHOOL BOARD'S NEW *INSTRUMENTS THAT ARE A DANGER TO STUDENT'S SAFETY* CATEGORY.

BANNED MUSICAL INSTRUMENTS

BUT... BUT...

I...

ISN'T IT TIME FOR CLASS?

YOU DON'T WANT A *TARDY SLIP* ON YOUR *PERMANENT RECORD*, DO YOU?

MY SAX. MY SAX.

LISA, STOP THAT *FINGERING!* IT'S DISTRACTING!

YOUR FRIEND SILENT "E"

MS. HOOVER? IS LISA *CRAZY?*

POSSIBLY, RALPH, BUT LIKE I TOLD YOU WHEN THE RABID SQUIRREL CAME IN THE WINDOW, THEY DON'T *PAY* ME ENOUGH TO *CARE*.

TODAY
ASS

MUMMY! DADDY! LOOK! I'M A *CLOWN!*

OH, PLEASE, CECIL. YOUR CLOWN DREAMS ARE MAKING YOU THE *LAUGHING STOCK* OF THE CUL DE SAC.

SMACK!

HA HA HA

NO! LOOK AT ME! LAUGH AT *ME*!

GASP! WHAT A DREADFUL *FLASHBACK-SLASH-NIGHTMARE*!

OH WELL, BACK TO EVIL!

GOT TO *CALM DOWN*. A TRIP TO THE LIBRARY. THE WORKS OF JAMES JOYCE, JUDY BLUME, AND THE BRIDGE BLOOPERS OF OMAR SHARIF WILL HELP *SETTLE MY NERVES*.

CLOSED FOR TOTAL RE-STOCKING

WHAT?

YES, WE WILL BE CLOSED WHILE I REPLACE ALL THE *OUT OF DATE, TEXT-BASED BOOKS* WITH THE SUPERIOR LITERATURE KNOWN AS *GRAPHIC NOVELS*. FROM AMAZING SPIDER-MAN TO ZATANNA.

YOU RUN THE LIBRARY NOW?

YES, A *BRILLIANT DECISION* BY THE NEW *FRIENDS OF THE LIBRARY COMMITTEE*. NOW GET YOUR GRUBBY LITTLE KID HANDS OFF OF THAT. THIS *ISN'T* A LIBRARY!

YES IT *IS*.

LIBRARY LAD

OH. WELL I...UM...

TOUCHÉ, LADY LISA, TOUCHÉ. YOU'VE WON *THIS* ROUND!

OH, HEY, I PUT YOUR *NEW THREAT-ENING LETTERS* ON YOUR BED.

THE LIBRARY IS *RUINED*.

NOW, LISA, THE DEWEY DECIMAL SYSTEM IS *FLAWED*, I'LL GIVE YOU THAT, BUT...

I DON'T GET IT! WHY WOULD SIDESHOW BOB SEND LETTERS TO *YOU* TO GET TO *ME*?

MAYBE THIS ISN'T ABOUT *YOU*. MAYBE HE'S AFTER *ME*!

HA, HA! YEAH, RIGHT!

WHAT? I'M NOT *IMPORTANT ENOUGH* TO HAVE A *MORTAL ENEMY*?

EXACTLY.

GRRRRRR. LET'S JUST WATCH "ITCHY AND SCRATCHY." I NEED TO RELAX.

HEY, HEY, KIDS! ITCHY AND SCRATCHY HAVE BEEN PERMANENTLY PUT ON *HIATUS*.

AND IT'S NOT BECAUSE SOMEONE'S *BLACKMAILING* ME WITH PICTURES FROM MY VACATION IN BANGKOK.

IN ITS PLACE, HERE'S SOME-THING JUST AS GOOD FROM ENGLAND. P.G. WODEHOUSE'S "JEEVES AND WOOSTER"!

I SAY, JEEVES, I'M IN A PICKLE. I HAVE A DATE WITH BOTH CECILY AND BEATRICE ON THE DAY I'M SUPPOSED TO MARRY THE QUEEN.

YOU, SIR, ARE A *BLOODY IDIOT*.

RATS! IT'S BASED ON ONE OF THE *LATER* NOVELS!

LISA, YOU'RE NOT EATING YOUR *TOFURKEY*.

SHE'S JUST *UPSET* BECAUSE SIDESHOW BOB IS ACCIDENTALLY SENDING MY DEATH THREATS TO HER.

OH, PLUS THE FACT THAT SHE'S LOST ALL THE THINGS THAT MAKE HER LIFE WORTHWHILE. *BOO-HOO!*

I CAN'T SAY I APPROVE OF EITHER OF YOU KIDS GETTING DEATH THREATHS. I'M GOING TO GET TO THE BOTTOM OF THIS!

NO, MRS. SIMPSON, SIDESHOW BOB IS *STILL HERE* IN THE EXERCISE YARD...

...AND OTHER THAN HIS WEEKLY LETTER TO "THE NEW YORK REVIEW OF BOOKS," BOB HASN'T SENT ANY MAIL AT ALL.

WE INTERRUPT THIS *DAY-LONG MOMENT OF SILENCE* FOR A *LIST OF THE SCHOOLS* THAT WILL BE *PERMANENTLY CLOSED* AS OF TOMORROW. *LISA SIMPSON'S SCHOOL.*

THAT IS ALL.

WOO-HOO!

NO SAX, NO BOOKS, NO CARTOONS, NO SCHOOL. *WHAT WILL I DO?*

18

LATER THAT NIGHT...

WAIT A MINUTE!

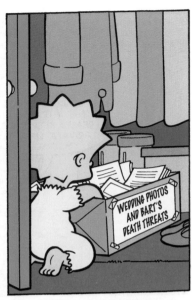

WEDDING PHOTOS AND BART'S DEATH THREATS

BART! WAKE UP!

THUD!

GLORP!

SORRY, LIS, I SET UP THAT BUCKET OF RANCID PUDDING TO TRAP BOB.

¡GASP!¡ WHY RANCID?

HOMER EATS LESS OF IT THEN.

LOOK AT BOB'S HANDWRITING ON THESE OLD DEATH THREATS OF YOURS. NOW LOOK AT THE NOTES I GOT. IT'S SIMILAR, BUT IT WASN'T WRITTEN BY THE SAME PERSON.

YOU'RE RIGHT!

19

IT'S ALMOST AS IF SOMEONE HAS FOUND OUT EVERYTHING THAT MAKES ME ME, AND IS *ELIMINATING* THEM ONE BY ONE. BUT HOW?

YEAH, ASIDE FROM THOSE PAGES OF YOUR DIARY I PUT ON THE INTERNET, YOU REALLY KEEP YOUR *PRIVATE LIFE* TO YOURSELF.

WHAT?!!!

WWW.STUPIDLISA-GARBAGEFACE.COM?! WE'LL TALK ABOUT THIS LATER.

IT'S GOT *ONE* HIT!

BUT WHY WOULD ANYONE TRY TO USE *YOU* TO GET TO *ME*?

ARE YOU EVEN *LISTENING* TO ME?

WHEN IT SEEMS LIKE YOU'RE TALKING ABOUT ME, YES. THE IDEA THAT SOMEONE'S TRYING TO GET *YOU*? I FIND THAT *HARD TO BELIEVE*.

CRAAASH!

I FIND IT SLIGHTLY LESS DIFFICULT TO BELIEVE.

MOM, DAD, A *WRECKING BALL* CAME THROUGH MY WALL, AND BART AND I ARE GOING TO *HUNT DOWN* THE PERSON WHO DID IT BEFORE THEY *DESTROY* ME!

TAKE A JACKET!

:SIGH!: WHY CAN'T I JUST *DREAM* ABOUT A *SHIRTLESS RAINIER WOLFCASTLE*? IT'S ALWAYS *THE KIDS IN DANGER*.

MMM...SHIRT-LESS RAINIER WOLFCASTLE.

SOON...

YES, LISA, WE TRACKED DOWN THE *I.P. ADDRESS* YOU GAVE US. THE USER IS AT 125 HIDEOUT RD. IN THE WAREHOUSE DISTRICT.

THE LONE GUNMEN TELEVISION SERIES 2001-2001

THANKS, GARY.

I'M BENJAMIN.

IS THERE *ANYTHING ELSE* YOU NEED? ANYTHING AT ALL? WE'RE SO *BORED*.

SINCE OUR DOT COM COMPANY FOLDED WE HAVE NOTHING TO DO BUT PLAY VIDEOGAMES AND EAT MICROWAVE SMORES.

SOON, AT THE WAREHOUSE DISTRICT...

THERE IT IS!

AND HERE *I* AM!

I FORGOT TO PUT CHLOROFORM ON THE RAGS, DIDN'T I?

!SIGH!

OKAY, JUST *WALK* TO THE HIDEOUT.

21

MINUTES LATER...

CECIL! I NEVER WOULD HAVE THOUGHT IT WAS *YOU!*

THIS IS AN AMAZING PLACE.

NO, NO ONE *EVER* THINKS OF *ME.*

YOU THINK SO? THANKS. IT'S A *RENTAL*, BUT I HOPE TO BUY ONCE MY CREDIT GETS A BIT BETTER.

SO, WHERE'S BOB?

IN JAIL I SUSPECT. HONESTLY, DO YOU *HAVE TO* BRING *HIM* UP? IT'S HARD ENOUGH ATTEMPTING TO GET OUT FROM YOUR *BROTHER'S* SHADOW.

EVEN THOUGH *YOU'RE* THE *SMARTER* ONE.

AMEN TO THAT!

BUT AS HARD AS YOU TRY, DO *YOU* EVER GET *ANY* ATTENTION?

NO!

WHICH IS WHY I PLANNED ALL THIS TO DESTROY *YOU*, LISA SIMPSON!

WHAT ABOUT *ME?*

WHAT *ABOUT* YOU? YOU'RE JUST A *SIDEKICK* WHO TAGGED ALONG.

TELL ME ABOUT *YOUR PLAN*. I'D LOVE TO HEAR IT.

WOULD YOU? BECAUSE I THINK YOU'D REALLY *UNDERSTAND* AND *APPRECIATE* IT.

I'M *BLUSHING.*

SIDEKICK?!!!

"I ASSUMED A *NEW IDENTITY* AND *INFILTRATED* A SCHOOL BOARD MEETING."

"FINDING ONLY *BORED BUREAUCRATS* WHO HAD LONG LOST THEIR PASSION FOR THE JOB, I QUICKLY *TOOK CHARGE*."

IT WAS *CHILD'S PLAY* TO BAN USE OF YOUR PRECIOUS SAX AND CLOSE YOUR SCHOOL.

I *REPEATED MY ACTIONS* WITH THE LIBRARY COMMITTEE. THE OWNER OF THE ANDROID'S DUNGEON WAS MORE THAN HAPPY WITH HIS NEW POSITION.

BLACKMAILING KRUSTY WAS A CINCH WITH SOME PICTURES DOWNLOADED BY MY *EASILY-BRIBED, COMPUTER CHATROOM CHUMS.*

BENJAMIN, DOUG, AND GARY?

NOTHING PERSONAL, LISA. LIKE WE SAID, WE WERE JUST *BORED.*

AND HERE IS YOUR *REWARD*. TICKETS TO THE BROADWAY PRODUCTION OF "WILLIAM SHATNER'S STAR TREK MEMORIES: THE MUSICAL," STARRING BATTLESTAR GALACTICA'S RICHARD HATCH! NOW OFF WITH YOU!

SO *FIRST*, YOU WANTED TO *BREAK MY SPIRIT*, AND THEN, WHEN I WAS AT MY *WEAKEST*, YOU SENT IN THE WRECKING BALL TO *FINISH ME OFF.*

WHAT WRECKING BALL?

WHY IS THE *CONSTRUCTION WORKERS' UNION* SO MAD AT YOU AGAIN?

I ATE THEIR LUNCHES.

I INTEND TO *FREEZE* YOU IN *LIQUID NITROGEN* AND *DISPLAY* YOU IN MY *REFRIGERATED TROPHY CASE.*

IN THE FUTURE, WHEN I NEED A *CHALLENGE* AGAIN, I SHALL *THAW YOU OUT.*

WOULD THAT WORK?

SO FAR THE PROCESS HAS BEEN 90% SUCCESSFUL. FOR SOME REASON THE DOOR TO DOOR SALESMEN *SHATTER* LIKE TIFFANY CRYSTAL.

CECIL, BEFORE YOU FREEZE ME I HAVE *ONE MORE QUESTION.*

IF IT'S MORE *BROTHER-BASHING,* THEN DIP ME NOW!

WHAT DO YOU FEEL IS THE *NUMBER ONE FLAW* MOST CRIMINAL MASTER-MINDS HAVE?

HMMMM, THAT'S A *POSER.* BUT I'D HAVE TO SAY *WASTING TIME* REVEALING THEIR PLANS ALLOWING HELP TO ARRIVE.

FREEZE, CECIL B. DE-BUSTED!

MAN, GOOD ONE CHIEF.

THANKS, EDDIE! I THOUGHT OF IT IN THE CAR ON THE WAY OVER. IT WASN'T *TOO MUCH?*

YOU CALLED THE POLICE BEFORE I CAUGHT YOU, AND YOU WERE JUST *STALLING* ME.

YES.

YOU TRULY ARE *BRILLIANT.* I CONSIDER MYSELF *HONORED* TO HAVE BEEN *BESTED* BY YOU, LISA.

WELL, MAYBE IT'S *THE STOCKHOLM SYNDROME* TALKING, BUT IF I HAVE TO HAVE A PSYCHO ARCH-ENEMY, THEN I'M GLAD HE'S YOU.

I'M NO *SIDESHOW BOB.*

HE'S NO *CECIL!*

OKAY. THIS IS *WEIRD*.

CAN WE JUST ARREST YOU NOW?

YES. TAKE ME AWAY, OFFICER.

HEY!

OH, SORRY. WE ALMOST FORGOT ABOUT...UM...

BART! I'M *BART*!

RIGHT! *LISA'S BROTHER*, BART.

LATER...

TERWILLIGER, THE WARDEN SAYS FOR THE *SAFETY* OF THE OTHER *NON-BRILLIANT, CRIMINAL MASTERMIND* PRISONERS, YOU HAVE TO SPEND THE NIGHT IN *SOLITARY*.

COME ALONG, CECIL.

I UNDER-STAND.

ME? SOLITARY?

HIM? I'M THE MASTER-MIND BROTHER HERE. WHAT ABOUT *ME*?

WHAT ABOUT *ME*?!!!

LISA SIMPSON - YOUR END IS NEAR.

BEST REGARDS YOUR MORTAL E...

THE END

Marge Simpson in
A RECIPE FOR DISASTER

I'M SORRY! I'M *SO* SORRY!

YOU ARE THE *EVIL* ONE! GET THEE *HENCE!*

YOU'VE TOTALLY *RUINED* THE CHURCH SOCIAL *POT LUCK* BY MAKING THE SAME, OLD THING!

THE SAME, OLD THING!

THE SAME, OLD THING!

≿GASP!≾ OH, HOMEY! I'VE JUST HAD THE *WORST NIGHTMARE!*

MAYBE MY *SUBCONSCIOUS* IS TRYING TO TELL ME SOMETHING ABOUT MY *COOKING!*

WELL, YOUR MEAT LOAF *HAS* BEEN A LITTLE *DRY* LATELY, AND YOUR PIES TOO *FLAKY.* OR IS IT THE OTHER WAY AROUND?

LUCKY FOR YOU, I HAVE THE *SOLUTION* TO YOUR PROBLEM *RIGHT HERE.*

I KEEP IT UNDER MY *PILLOW,* CLOSE TO MY *HEART!*

JESSE L. MCCANN & SERAN WILLIAMS
SCRIPT

KIM LE
PENCILS

MIKE ROTE
INKS

ART VILLANUEVA
COLORS

KAREN BATES
LETTERS

BILL MORRISON
EDITOR

MATT GROENING
HAPPY HOMEMAKER

CHIEF WIGGUM'S PADDY-WAGON-CAKE

OH, MY! THAT'S TOO *WEIRD*...AND *DANGEROUS*.

SAY...MAYBE I SHOULD MAKE A *DESSERT*...

WHY *SERVE TIME* WHEN YOU CAN SERVE THIS TASTY *NOVELTY TREAT*?

INGREDIENTS:
1 (18.25 ounce) package white cake mix
5 tablespoons crème de menthe flavoring
1 (16 ounce) can chocolate syrup
1 (8 ounce) container frozen whipped topping, thawed
1 pair freshly scrubbed handcuffs, key set aside

PREPARATION:
Prepare 1 box white cake mix as directed, except substitute 3 tablespoons crème de menthe flavoring for 3 tablespoons water. Pour into 13x9 inch pan and drop handcuffs into batter.

1.

WHEN I DO THIS PART, I LIKE TO SHOUT, "FREEZE, SCUMBAG! I BELIEVE THESE *BRACELETS* ARE YOURS!"

I ALWAYS GET A *KICK* OUT OF THAT.

DECORATE WITH SOME OF THOSE *CUTE* LITTLE *COLOR SPRINKLES* THAT I LOVE SO MUCH!

2.

Bake according to cake package directions. Remove from oven and while hot, poke holes in cake with fork, then pour chocolate syrup over the top. Refrigerate until cool, about one hour. After cooling, mix whipped topping with 2 tablespoons of crème de menthe and spread on cake.

3.

Keep refrigerated or put in freezer till ready to serve. Makes 1-13x19 inch sheet cake. Tell whoever finds the 'cuffs that they're "Busted." Ha! It's a great party joke, especially at political fund-raisers!

HANDCUFFS *INSIDE* A CAKE? I DON'T EVEN WANT TO THINK ABOUT THE POTENTIAL *DENTIST BILLS*!

MANY FOLKS THINK IT'S AN *EXCELLENT* CAKE TO BAKE WHEN A LOVED ONE IS IN THE *HOOSEGOW*. THEY JUST SUBSTITUTE A *FILE* FOR THE HANDCUFFS, REMEMBERING TO AVOID *METAL DETECTORS*!

BUT DON'T TRY IT DURING *MY* WATCH! I'D BE ON TO YOU *FASTER* THAN *MOLASSES* ON A *PANCAKE*, PAL!

OH, LOOK! *HOMER'S* GOT A RECIPE IN THIS BOOK!

HOMER'S BEER BISCUITS

THE *BEER* MAKES 'EM BETTER!

INGREDIENTS:
1 case of Duff Beer
2 cups sifted all-purpose flour
4 tsp baking powder
1 tsp salt
1/4 cup shortening
3/4 cup milk

SO I SAYS TO THE *COOK,* I SAYS TO 'IM, "YOU THINK YOU'RE SO *GREAT?* YOU THINK *I* CAN'T MAKE...*FOOD,* TOO?"

1.

PREPARATION:
Drink a can of Duff. Sift dry ingredients together. Cut in shortening. Drink half of a can of Duff. Pour the rest of the can of Duff into the mixture. Drink another can of Duff so you won't regret wasting the previous half-can of Duff. Turn out the dough on a lightly floured board. Knead about 1/2 minute. During this 1/2 minute, why not enjoy another Duff?

SO *HE* SAYS...HE *TELLS* ME...WHAT WAS I TALKIN' ABOUT?

...ZZZZZZ!

3.

Invite some friends over, but make sure they bring their own Duff. By the time you're done with all that hot and strenuous phone-calling, you'll probably need another Duff. If you forget the biscuits and they burn, throw them out and drink the rest of the Duff. If the biscuits turn out good, serve them with something thirst-quenching. I recommend a cold and friendly stein of Duff!

2.
Roll out dough 1/2 inch thick. Cut with floured biscuit cutter. You'll probably wound yourself with the cutter, so it's time for another wonderful Duff! Place dough cut-outs on baking sheet and bake in 475∞ f oven 12-15 minutes. Now, open a Duff and wait.

OH, THE *HECK* WITH IT! I'LL JUST *MAKE* SOME OF THESE RECIPES AND *HOPE* FOR THE *BEST!*

WHAT'S THE *WORST* THAT COULD HAPPEN?

BEER IN THE LORD'S HOUSE?! GET THEE HENCE, *EVIL ONE!!*

I'M *SO* SORRY!

MOTHER *CHIPPED* A *TOOTH!*

YOUR *COCONUT* GAVE ME A *CONCUSSION!*

THE END

29

IT'S A *FUNNY STORY*, REALLY. MILHOUSE WANTED TO LEARN HOW TO PLAY *CRICKET*, BUT IT WAS GOING KINDA *SLOW*.

SO BART THOUGHT, WHY NOT USE A *SUPERBALL* AND...

YOU BROKE SAINT IGNATIUS, SAINT SEBASTIAN, AND EVEN POOR SAINT OLAF!

HOW'S SAINT PTOLOMAEUS?

LIKE THE OTHERS, I'M SURE HE DEMANDS *SWIFT* AND *HARSH* VENGEANCE!

OR IN LIEU OF VENGEANCE...

...$2,000 DOLLARS!?

I SUPPOSE WE'LL JUST HAVE TO *CUT BACK* ON *LUXURIES*.

EVERYONE POUR THEIR *GRAVY* BACK INTO THE *BOAT*. C'MON! C'MON!

AND SO...

YOU KNOW, MOM, THAT *BARGAIN HAIR DYE* LOOKS FINE.

I DIDN'T THINK I'D LIKE *SKY BLUE*, BUT I'M GETTING USED TO IT.

OH, THE PAPER'S HERE!

THUD!

OH, DEAR LORD!

HA, HA!

MOM, THERE ARE *BIRDS* STUCK IN YOUR--

QUIET, LISA. YOUR MOTHER HAS TO "HRMMM" NOW.

HRMMM...

ON *THE BRIGHT SIDE*, MAGGIE SURE LIKES HER *NEW PACIFIER*.

WE GOT IT *FREE* IN THE MAIL FROM *LARAMIE CIGARETTES*.

SUCK! SUCK!

DAD, THESE ARE ALMOST *PURE NICOTINE*.

Laramie
98.9% NICOTEEN

OF COURSE, THEY'RE *PURE*, HONEY. *BABY THINGS* HAVE TO BE *SAFE*.

BUT...

SUCK! SUCK!

YOU'RE JUST *GRUMPY* BECAUSE WE HAD TO *PAWN* YOUR SAXAMAPHONE FOR A WHILE.

WHY AREN'T YOU *PRACTICING* WITH THE ONE THE SCHOOL *LENT* YOU?

HERE YOU GO, LISA!

UNFORTUNATELY THE SPIT VALVE'S *JAMMED*.

WE HAVEN'T BEEN ABLE TO *EMPTY IT* SINCE THE FIFTIES.

EWWW!

THAT FALCON IS *AMAZING*. I'VE TOTALLY FORGOTTEN WHY I WAS MAD AT YOU, BOY.

BART COST YOU $2,000 DOLLARS.

OH, RIGHT.

WHY YOU LITTLE...!

¡GAAK!¡

SCREEEE!

AAAAAH! FALCON!

THE NEXT DAY...

HEY, THANKS FOR THE LIFT, GUYS. I CAN'T AFFORD *GAS* RIGHT NOW.

HEY, THANK *YOU* FOR THE EXTRA HELPING OF *DEODORANT*.

SO, LENNY, CARL, YOU GUYS RIDE TO WORK TOGETHER *EVERYDAY*?

YEP.

AND *CARPOOLING* DOESN'T MAKE YOU FEEL LIKE *LOSERS*?

NO? WHY SHOULD IT?

NO REASON. I MEAN THE *CARPOOL LANE*. HEH, HEH. NOTHING'S *COOLER* THAN THE *CARPOOL LANE*.

THAT'S IT! I TOLD YOU HE COULDN'T GO A *MILE* WITHOUT MAKING A *DEROGATORY COMMENT*. THIS WAS A *MISTAKE*.

WHAT ARE YOU TALKING ABOUT? I'M JUST CALLING YOU *LOSERS* FOR *CARPOOLING* IS ALL.

GEEZ! YOU *CARPOOLING LOSERS* SURE ARE *SENSITIVE*.

WELL, AT LEAST WE "LOSERS" NEVER HAVE TO *WORK* AGAIN AFTER NEXT WEEK.

YEP. SWEET, SWEET *RETIREMENT*.

WHAT THE HELL ARE YOU TALKING ABOUT?

YOU CAN'T RETIRE. YOU'RE NOT *OLD*!

YOU DIDN'T READ THE *MEMO*?

WHAT AM I SAYING? *OF COURSE* YOU DIDN'T.

MR. BURNS DECIDED HE WANTS TO KEEP THE COMPANY *YOUNG* AND *VIBRANT*.

SO HE'S GIVING US THE OPTION OF *RETIRING AT FORTY* AND LIVING ON A *HAWAIIAN ISLAND*, RENT-FREE, FOR *THE REST OF OUR LIVES*.

I WANT TO RETIRE, TOO!

YOU GOTTA BE *FORTY*.

LATER...

YOU WERE *BORN* IN *1941*? THIS *I.D.* LOOKS *FAKE*.

OH, AND NEXT YOU'LL *ACCUSE ME* OF MAKING A *FAKE I.D.* IN THE EIGHTIES TO GET OUT OF FIGHTING IN *THE COLA WARS*.

38

EXCUSE ME.

HERE'S YOUR WATER.

IT'S GOT YOU ON A *PAGER*?

YEAH. I HAVE TO DO *EVERYTHING* FOR HIM. WHAT A *STUPID BIRD*.

THE NEXT DAY...

ZZZZZ!

YAAAH!

HURRY UP, HOMER.

YEAH, TODAY'S *THE BIG DAY!*

GREETINGS, *OLD TIMERS,* AND WELCOME TO *KAROUSEL!* PLEASE NOTE THE SPELLING OF KAROUSEL WITH A *"K"* TO AVOID *COPYRIGHT INFRINGEMENT*.

LET YOUR ⸨HEH, HEH⸩ *RETIREMENT* BEGIN!

CLICK!

CLICK!

SMITHERS, WHY WEREN'T THEY *FLOATING INTO THE AIR* AND *EXPLODING*?

THE *UNION* WOULDN'T *ALLOW* IT, SIR.

VERY WELL THEN. GIVE THEM THEIR *PLANE TICKETS* AND HAVE THE *HIRED GOONS* ESCORT THEM OUT OF THE BUILDING.

HEY, YOU'RE *TWISTING MY ARM* THE WRONG WAY.

OH, SORRY. IT'S HIS *FIRST DAY* OUT OF *GOON SCHOOL*.

PACK YOUR BAGS! THE SIMPSONS ARE *GOING TO HAWAII!*

THAT'S *WONDERFUL!*

YAY!

OKAY, AS SOON AS I FINISH FALCO'S *FOOT MASSAGE*.

43

:COUGH!: :COUGH!: ANY *PLANES* SEE OUR *TRASH FIRE*?

NO. :COUGH!: :COUGH!: BART, I'M *WORRIED* WE'LL NEVER GET *RESCUED*.

THAT'S NO WAY TO TALK, *LITTLE BUDDIES*!

HEY, HOMER, WHERE DID YOU FIND THE *BLUE SHIRT*?

WE'RE *CAST-AWAYS*, AND IF WE'RE GONNA STAY *SANE*, WE HAVE TO START HAVING *WACKY ADVENTURES*.

I'LL BE *THE SKIPPER*.

BART, YOU'RE *GILLIGAN*.

LISA, YOU'RE THE *PROFESSOR*. MAGGIE, *MARY ANN*.

CARL, YOU'RE *THE HARLEM GLOBE-TROTTERS*!

NOW, LET'S HIDE! THERE ARE *HEADHUNTERS* EVERYWHERE, A *GIANT SPIDER*, AND A GUY WHO DOESN'T KNOW *WORLD WAR II* IS OVER.

HA HA HA HA HA HA

I'M *WORRIED* ABOUT HOMER.

I'M *MORE WORRIED* ABOUT WHERE THAT *LAUGH TRACK* IS COMING FROM.

HA HA HA HA HA HA

IT'S *BART'S* PAGER!

SO? FALCO CAN GET HIS OWN BLANKET.

I MAY BE ABLE TO *REVERSE THE WIRING* SO WE CAN SEND AN *S.O.S. MESSAGE* WITH OUR *LOCATION.*

BEEP! BEEEEEP! BEEP!

SEEDS

LATER...

MAYBE IT'S JUST THE *ISLAND MADNESS* TALKING, BUT THAT MARGE SURE IS PRETTY. I THINK I'LL *DROWN* HOMER AND MAKE HER MY *BRIDE.* WANNA HELP?

OKAY, BUT THEN I'LL DROWN *YOU* AND MAKE HER *MY* BRIDE LATER.

FAIR ENOUGH.

WAIT A MINUTE. HOW DO I KNOW YOU GUYS WON'T *CHEAT* AT THIS *BREATH HOLD-ING CONTEST?*

LOOK, WE'LL TIE THESE *BAGS OF CEMENT* TO YOU TO GIVE YOU A *HEAD START.*

CEMENT

SCREEEE!

WHAT THE--?

MAN, IT GETS DARK EARLY HERE.

46

LATER...

I HOPE YOU'RE ALL HAPPY WITH YOUR-SELVES. ALL MY PRECIOUS *TAX DEDUCTIBLE GARBAGE,* GONE!

YOU KNOW YOU *DID* TRICK US WITH THAT *PHONY RETIREMENT*.

NO *SPEAKING* WHILE MR. BURNS IS *RANTING!*

YOU'LL PAY! OH YES, YOU'LL ALL...

...SMITHERS, WHO IS THIS *NOBLE CREATURE?*

IT APPEARS TO BE A *FALCON,* SIR.

HE'S FALCO.

FALCO, EH? I LIKE *THE CUT OF HIS GIBLETS*.

HE REMINDS ME OF *MYSELF*.

YOU CAN HAVE HIM...

REALLY?

...IF YOU GIVE MY DAD, LENNY, AND CARL THEIR JOBS BACK.

PLUS $2,000 DOLLARS!

AGREED!

A WEEK LATER...

I'VE GOT TO SAY, IT'S NICE TO HAVE OUR *LUXURIES* BACK AGAIN.

MY HAIR'S BACK TO NORMAL, AND I THINK MAGGIE MISSES HER *LARAMIE PACIFIERS*, BUT I'M SURE SHE'LL GET OVER IT.

HOW ABOUT YOU, HOMIE? HOW'S WORK?

IT'S *GREAT!* THINGS ARE WAY *MORE EFFICIENT*, AND I'VE *DOUBLED* MY *NAPPING* AND *SNACK TIME!*

I REALLY THINK YOU'RE LETTING THAT FALCON HAVE *TOO MUCH POWER*, SIR.

HAVE YOU SEEN THE *NEW PROFIT REPORTS?* WE'RE UP 75%!

WHATEVER FALCO'S DOING, IT'S WORKING.

BUT, SIR--!

50

THE END

IN MY TRAVELS, I AM OFTEN ASKED BY MY MANY ADMIRERS--WHAT LED ME TO MY CURRENT *EXALTED POSITION* AS AMERICA'S *MOST REVERED* AND *BELOVED SIDEKICK* IN THE CRUCIAL 6-10 YEAR OLD DEMOGRAPHIC? WELL, SIT DOWN, DEAR READER, AND *PREPARE YOURSELF* FOR THE

SECRET ORIGIN OF SIDESHOW MEL!

LONG AGO AT THE SPRINGFIELD SPEEDWAY...

...THE MOST *ASTOUNDING VICTORY* THIS REPORTER HAS EVER *SEEN!*

CAR 2'S DRIVER, IN A *STUNNING* DISPLAY OF *COURAGE*, HAS *FINISHED THE RACE* IN *FIRST PLACE*, DESPITE HIS CAR BEING *ENGULFED IN FLAMES!*

IF HE'S STILL *ALIVE*, THAT'S REALLY *INTERESTING!*

QUICK! TRY TO SAVE THE *ESPRESSO MACHINE!*

DID I NOT *REQUEST* THAT YOU *ADJUST* THE VALANCE, THUS INCREASING THE *FRONT DOWNFORCE*, WORTHY PIT CREW *CAPTAIN?*

SORRY, MR. VAN HORNE...

I VERY NEARLY *SINGED MY BONE!*

GAIL SIMONE
STORY

RYAN RIVETTE
PENCILS

ANDREW PEPOY
INKS

ART VILLANUEVA
COLORS

KAREN BATES
LETTERS

BILL MORRISON
EDITOR

MATT GROENING
SECOND TO NONE

53

...AND THEN, I BECAME ONLY THE **SECOND MAN** TO CLIMB THE TALLEST PEAKS ON EACH CONTINENT...

YEAH? ANY **SELTZER** EXPERIENCE? WHAT ABOUT **CANNONS**--WHAT ARE YOUR FEELINGS ON BEING **SHOT OUT OF THEM?**

WELL, NO, I MUST CONFESS MY EXPERIENCE IS MORE IN THE REALMS OF THE **FINE ARTS** AND **MICRO-BIOLOGY**...

LOOK...KID...I'M LOOKING FOR A SIDEKICK WITH **EXPERIENCE,** YA KNOW? IF IT WEREN'T FOR SIDESHOW BOB, SIDESHOW RAGHIB, AND SIDESHOW LUKE PERRY ALL BEING IN **JAIL,** WE WOULDN'T EVEN BE **TALKING** RIGHT NOW!

KRUSTY, PLEASE, I **BESEECH** YOU! IF YOU GIVE ME JUST **ONE CHANCE,** I **KNOW** I CAN BE THE **BUFFOON** THAT VIEWERS WILL LOVE TO SEE YOU **ABUSE** AND **HUMILIATE!**

WELL, I DON'T KNOW...HE MAKES A **GOOD PITCH,** AND THE **BONE THING** IS BOFFO!

OOH OOH EEE AH AHH!

AW, YOU **ALWAYS** SAY THAT.

AND **STAY OUTTA MY CUBANS!**

SWIPE!

ALL RIGHT, KID. YOU GET **ONE SHOT** TONIGHT, LIVE, ON THE SHOW. IF ANYONE LAUGHS, YOU **KEEP THE GIG.** IF NOT, I'M GONNA HAVE TO GO WITH **SIDESHOW BILL SHATNER.**

KRUUSTTEEEE! LET **ME**...TAKE... THE **PIE!** IN THE... FAAAAACE!

OH, **THANK** YOU, KRUSTY! YOU **SHAN'T** REGRET THIS!

CRIPES! NOW MY **STOGIE** TASTES LIKE **MONKEY!**

...UNLESS YOU'RE *SELLING* THEM SPRINGFIELD ELEMENTARY SCHOOL *CHOCOLATE!*

REMEMBER, CHILDREN, YOU'RE *REQUIRED* TO SELL AS MUCH CANDY AS YOU CAN TO HELP *RAISE FUNDS* FOR THE SCHOOL.

EXCEPT, FOR OBVIOUS REASONS, UTER!

LET ME AT DER CHOCOLATE! I BEG YOU!

YES, LISA? YOU HAVE A QUESTION?

PRINCIPAL SKINNER, WHAT DOES THE MONEY GO TOWARDS? NEW BOOKS? FIELD TRIPS?

AHEM, YES. IF THERE'S ANY MONEY LEFT OVER AFTER PAYING FOR SOME MUCH NEEDED *IMPROVEMENTS* TO THE *TEACHER'S LOUNGE*.

TEACHERS LOUNGE

♪ WE'RE HOT ♪ TUBBING, CHECK US AND SEE! OUR BODY TEMPERATURE'S ♪ 103! ♪

AND REMEMBER, *FIRST PRIZE* FOR WHICHEVER STUDENT SELLS THE MOST CHOCOLATE IS...

...HAVING YOUR *PERMANENT RECORD INCINERATED*.

I'D FINALLY BE ABLE TO PUT THAT "B+" BEHIND ME.

I *FEEL* FOR YOU, LIS.

LATER...

I THINK I'LL START IN RICHDALE AND WORK MY WAY TO JUNKIEVILLE AND BUMTOWN.

I'M GOING HOME FIRST.

WHAT? WHY?

A *NEW PROBE* HAS LANDED ON *MARS,* AND I WANT TO WATCH THE *LIVE FOOTAGE.*

GIVE ME A HEADS UP IF THE *MARTIANS* ARE PLANNING TO *INVADE!*

YOU GOT IT!

WILLIE! UTER'S FREE! CODE RED! *CODE RED!*

I'LL GET THE *TASER GUN!*

AND SO YOU SEE, MARS' SURFACE IS PRETTY DUSTY. WE'RE READING AN ATMOSPHERE OF 95% CARBON DIOXIDE AND 2% ARGON.

FASCINATING.

BUT I WANTED TO SEE THAT SHOW WHERE GOOD-LOOKING PEOPLE GET COVERED IN RATS.

AN INTERESTING FACT, THE MARS ROVER CAN MOVE UP TO 15 KILOMETERS AN HOUR.

AW... AND THERE'S *METRIC.*

???

DO YOU THINK *I* COULD EVER GO INTO SPACE, DAD?

WHY NOT? *I DID.* YOU SHOULD HAVE SAID SOME-THING. I WOULD HAVE *SMUGGLED* YOU ON BOARD.

MADRE DIOS! *THE MOTHER LOAD!*

I'M PLEASED THAT MY *MEAGER COLLECTION* OF TELEVISION, MOVIE AND COMIC MEMORABILIA *IMPRESSES* YOU.

AND BY MEAGER I MEAN *THE LARGEST IN THE WORLD.*

BUT WHERE ARE MY MANNERS? IT IS TIME I REVEALED MYSELF!

WOW! IT'S *YOU!* I DON'T BELIEVE IT!

YOU HAVE NO IDEA WHO I AM, DO YOU?

NO, SORRY.

≥SIGH.≤

I'M *CORNELIUS MORGAN*. FOR OVER *FIFTY YEARS* I PUBLISHED *"DISTINGUISHED MONSTER MONTHLY,"* A MAGAZINE DEDICATED TO ALL THINGS FANTASY, HORROR, AND SCIENCE FICTION.

AN *ACTUAL* SPACE MUTANTS TENTACLE. *COOOOL!*

D.M.M.

IS THAT A *REAL* RADIO-ACTIVE MAN OUTFIT?

YES, IN 1967 I *DIRECTED* THE RADIOACTIVE MAN *MOVIE*, BASED ON THE CAMP TELEVISION SHOW.

NO WAY!

WAY *INDEED*, DEAR BOY. WAY INDEED!

ATOMIC BOMB

CLICK

ATOMIC BOMB

TICK! TICK! TICK!

ATOMIC BOMB

ABE LINCOLN LOOK-ALIKE CONTEST

TICK! ATOMIC BOMB TICK! TICK!

IT SURE IS *HARDER* THAN YOU'D THINK TO GET RID OF *AN ATOMIC BOMB!*

ATOMIC BOMB

BOOM!

UH-OH!

THERE'S ONLY ONE THING TO DO NOW. HIT IT, *PAUL REVERE AND THE RAIDERS!*

EVERYONE, DO *"THE RADIOACTIVE-ATUSI"!*

MEANWHILE...

THANKS FOR DRIVING ME TO SHELBYVILLE, DAD. ALL OUR NEIGHBORS BOUGHT CANDY *ALREADY* FROM THE OTHER KIDS.

HEY, IT'S EITHER *THIS* OR *GO BACK TO WORK* AND CLEAN UP THAT *TOXIC SPILL* I CAUSED.

ARE YOU SURE YOU DON'T WANT TO BUY A BOX?

SCHOOL CANDY? EEEEEW!

IT'D TASTE ALL *EDUCATIONAL*!

UH...DAD. WE'RE NOT ON THE ROAD ANYMORE.

RELAX, DADDY KNOWS A *SHORTCUT*.

CRUNCH!

UH-OH.

DAD! YOU *RAN OVER* SOMETHING!

OH MY GOSH! IT LOOKS LIKE *THE MARS ROVER*!

CUT! CUT! WHO LET THE CAR ONTO THE LOCATION?

THEY'RE ⸬GASP⸬ *FAKING* THE *LIVE SPACE FOOTAGE*!

MEANWHILE...

WITH ALL THIS STUFF YOU MUST BE THE *HAPPIEST GUY ALIVE.*

SO YOU WOULD THINK, BUT ALAS, SOON *MY LIFE*, LIKE ALL *GREAT ADVENTURES*, MUST *FADE TO BLACK.*

YOU'RE *DYING?*

I WISH. IN ONE WEEK I'M BEING *CRYOGENICALLY FROZEN* AND *PUT ON DISPLAY* IN A COMIC SHOP IN SEATTLE.

WHY?

IT WAS PART OF MY *CONTRACT* WHEN I DIRECTED AN EPISODE OF "SLIDERS." I HAD A *VERY BAD AGENT.*

BUT I DON'T REGRET THAT. MY ONLY SADNESS IS THAT I HAVE *NO ONE* TO *LEAVE* ALL MY COMIC BOOKS, NOVELS, MOVIE AND TELEVISION PROPS TO.

I'LL TAKE 'EM!

NO, MY DEAR BOY. YOU SEE, FOR YEARS I WAS *SPRINGFIELD'S BIGGEST NERD.*

MY COLLECTION MUST GO TO WHO-EVER CAN TAKE THAT *MANTLE* FROM ME WHEN I'M GONE.

WHY NOT HAVE A *CONTEST* TO FIND THE TOWN'S *NEW* BIGGEST NERD?

BRILLIANT! YOU HAVE THE MIND OF A YOUNG ME, BEFORE I DESTROYED IT THOUGH YEARS OF *OPIUM SMOKING* AND *BINGE EATING.*

NOW, IF YOU'LL EXCUSE ME, I NEED SOME ALONE TIME.

TEN MINUTES LATER...

...AND SO THIS REPORTER WISHES THE CITY'S NERDS GOOD LUCK! *MAY THE BEST GEEK WIN!*

WOW!

THAT COLLECTION *MUST* BE MINE!

NO! EGA-HOYVEN! SUCH *TREASURES!* I MUST HAVE THEM IN MY PALE, SWEATY HANDS.

HEY, YOU NERDS, EITHER BUY SOMETHING OR QUIT BLOCKING MY WINDOW!

GAAAH!

FRANKLY I DON'T EVEN KNOW WHY WE WERE ALL WATCHING THAT TOGETHER.

WHAT I DO KNOW IS *THE GAUNTLET HAS BEEN THROWN DOWN* AND *THE CONTEST IS ON!*

FINE. WE ALL HAVE OUR *OWN* TVS ANYWAY!

BACK IN THE DESERT...

YOU *FAKE* SPACE FOOTAGE HERE?

FAKE IS SUCH A *HARSH WORD*. *ACCURATE*, BUT HARSH.

AND BESIDES...

THWACK!

OW!

MR. SIMPSON, PLEASE LEAVE THE *GOLF CLUBS* ON THE *MOON SET* ALONE!

SORRY!

PERHAPS *I* CAN EXPLAIN. YOU SEE, LISA, TWO-THIRDS OF SPACE MISSIONS *FAIL MISERABLY*. AND PEOPLE FEEL *UNCOMFORTABLE* WHEN A *TEN BILLION DOLLAR PROBE* THEIR TAXES PAID FOR *DOESN'T QUITE MAKE IT* TO MARS.

SO WHEN *SOMETHING GOES WRONG*, WE JUST POP ON OUT TO THE DESERT, SHOOT SOME FOOTAGE OF WHAT *SHOULD HAVE HAPPENED*, AND *EVERYBODY'S HAPPY*.

YOU WANT PEOPLE TO BE *HAPPY*, DON'T YOU, LISA?

BACK AT THE SIMPSON HOUSE...

HEY, BART, WHAT ARE YOU DOING FOR THE BIG CONTEST?

I THOUGHT I'D BUILD A *FIFTY-FOOT RADIOACTIVE MAN* OUT OF *MATCHSTICKS*.

COOL.

THEN I STARTED *WATCHING TV* AND *EATING CHIPS*.

AND?

THAT'S IT.

LATER INSIDE THE KRUSTYBURGER...

FELLOW *SUPERFRIENDS!* WE MUST *RISE TO THE CHALLENGE* OF PROVING OUR *NERDISHNESS!*

HOW ABOUT A DUNGEONS AND DRAGONS-STYLE *QUEST?*

BUT FOR WHAT?

WHILE ON THE ROAD OUTSIDE THE KRUSTYBURGER...

AW, MAN, THIS BOOK DOESN'T HAVE ANYTHING TO DO WITH *TOKING!*

WHAT A WASTE OF A TREE!

TOLKIEN

WELL, KENT, *MY* INVENTION WILL COME TO THE AID OF NERDS WHO DON'T HAVE TIME TO READ ALL THE *SCI-FI TRILOGIES* OUT THERE.

IT'S CALLED...*THE MONONIZER!*

IT *COMBINES THREE BOOKS INTO ONE* BY NOT MAKING WITH THE SUBPLOTS, THE EXPO-SITION, AND EGA-HA-HOYE FORESHADOWING.

AMAZING! DOES IT WORK ON MOVIES TOO?

BIG BOOK OF DUNE

I USED IT ON MY "STAR WARS TRILOGY" VIDEOS THIS MORNING.

OBI-WAN, YOU'RE MY ONLY HOPE AND BY THE WAY DARTH VADER IS MY FATHER.

I'D HELP YA OUT, LUKE, BUT I'M STUCK IN CARBONITE. NO WAIT, I'M OUT.

YAHOO! I BLEW UP *ALL* THE DEATH STARS!

FOR YEARS, KENT, COMPUTER NERDS HAVE TRIED TO *MERGE* THE INTERNET WITH EVERY-DAY LIVES.

BUT FOR SOME REASON NORMAL PEOPLE DON'T SEEM TO CARE.

SO WE DECIDED TO BRING THE INTERNET TO REAL LIFE. IN WHAT WE CALL *BIO-CONVERGENCE*.

SO ASIDE FROM PAINTING THE LAWN IN THIS PARK BLUE AND KILL-ING IT FOREVER, WHAT HAVE YOU DONE?

WELL, LET'S GIVE A QUESTION TO GARY, OUR *SEARCH ENGINE*.

I'M GOING TO SEE "THELMA AND LOUISE 3" TONIGHT, WHEN DOES IT START?

GO SEARCH ENGINE, GO!

OW! QUIT IT!

WHAT TIME DOES "THELMA AND LOUISE 3" START TONIGHT?

JAB!

UH...LET ME SEE. 7:00 AND 9:30.

IT *WORKS!* HUZZAH!

HEY, CAN I HAVE A MINUTE OF YOUR TIME TO TELL YOU ABOUT A *PYRAMID SCHEME* THAT REALLY WORKED FOR ME?

UH-OH! *SPAM!*

COUGH!

AND A *VIRUS!*

HE'S DONE FOR!

RUN!

MEANWHILE...

MOM, HOW *IMPORTANT* IS THE TRUTH?

THE TRUTH IS VERY IMPORTANT, LISA. YOU CAN'T LIVE A LIE.

BUT IF YOU DO, YOU'VE GOT TO *KEEP SMILING* AND *ACCEPT YOUR CHOICES.* THERE'S *NO TURNING BACK* NOW!

UM... MOM?

I LOVE YOUR FATHER, AND THAT'S ALL THERE IS TO IT! *END OF DISCUSSION!*

SLAM!

NOW, GO CALL BART AND HOMER! I'VE GOT TO *WASTE MY LIFE.*

WHAT?

I MEAN...I'VE GOT TO *WASH MY KNIFE.* YES, THAT'S IT.

THE NEXT DAY...

HEY, LISA. DID YOU *RAT OUT* N.A.S.A. YET?

HI, DAD.

NO. I STILL FEEL *GUILTY* ABOUT *NOT* TELLING THE TRUTH, BUT I THINK I'D FEEL *MORE* GUILTY IF I DID. IT'S SO *FRUSTRATING!*

DON'T WORRY, HONEY. IN THIRTEEN YEARS YOU CAN *DRINK BEER.*

IT *WASHES* ALL THE *GUILT BRAIN CELLS* AWAY.

THIS IS SCOTT CHRISTIAN SUBSTITUTING FOR KENT BROCKMAN, WHO IS ON VACATION.

WE TAKE YOU NOW TO *MORE* LIVE FOOTAGE FROM MARS. DR. BABCOCK, CAN YOU TELL US WHAT WE'RE SEEING?

YES, SCOTT. THINGS SEEM TO BE GOING *JUST AS PLANNED* WITH *NO UNEXPECTED PROBLEMS.*

UH-OH.

EXCUSE ME, DOCTOR, BUT DOES THAT SAY "HOMER RULES?"

NO! DEFINITELY NOT! IT'S JUST SOME, UH...*NATURAL EROSION.*

WOO-HOO! EVEN ON MARS, *I RULE!*

WAY TO GO, DAD!

GREETINGS, FELLOW NERDS! I HAVE GATHERED YOU HERE AT MY MANSION TO ANNOUNCE *THE VICTOR* OF THE CONTEST!

AND THE WINNER IS...

...ME!

WHAT KIND OF *"UNBREAKABLE"*-STYLE *TWIST ENDING* IS THIS?

FOR YEARS I HAVE LONGED TO MAKE *ANOTHER MOVIE*. TO SHOW *HOLLYWOOD* I STILL HAD WHAT IT TAKES.

AND NOW WITH THE HELP OF KENT BROCKMAN...

...AND YOUR *KIND, UNWITTING ASSISTANCE,* I'VE DONE IT!

NERDTOWN U.S.A.
A MOCKUMENTARY

SO YOU WEREN'T *INTERVIEWING* US FOR *THE NEWS*?

NO, WE JUST USED THAT AS AN EXCUSE TO FILM YOUR *RIDICULOUS ANTICS*. THIS JUST IN, IT WAS *HILARIOUS*!

I FEEL SO *BETRAYED*. IF MY CONTACT LENSES ALLOWED IT, I WOULD *WEEP!*

BUT WE SPENT THE WHOLE WEEK MAKING THIS *WORKING REPLICA* OF A *ROBO-TECHNO-GUNDAM MISSILE LAUNCHER BOT.*

AND YOU HAVE MY *SINCERE THANKS* FOR ALL YOU'VE DONE. I'D ADVISE YOU ALL NOW TO LEAVE *MY PROPERTY* AND GET YOURSELVES *SOME LIVES.*

GRRRR!

WHAP!

TARGET...ACQUIRED.

RUUUUMBLE!

SWEET JONATHAN FRAKE'S BEARD! IT'S *ACTIVATED! RUN!*

KA-BLAM!

CHRIS YAMBAR
STORY

KIM LE
PENCILS

JAMES HUANG
INKS

ART VILLANUEVA
COLORS

KAREN BATES
LETTERS

BILL MORRISON
EDITOR

MATT GROENING
BIKINI INSPECTOR

SEPTEMBER: FIRST DAY OF SCHOOL.

SPRINGFIELD
ELEMENTARY
SCHOOL

BBRRRIIINNNNGGGG!

Aa Bb Cc Dd Ee Ff Gg Hh Ii Jj Kk Ll Mm Nn O

REPORT: WHAT I DID ON
MY SUMMER VACATION

SCRITCH
SCRITCH

?

FLIP!

THE END

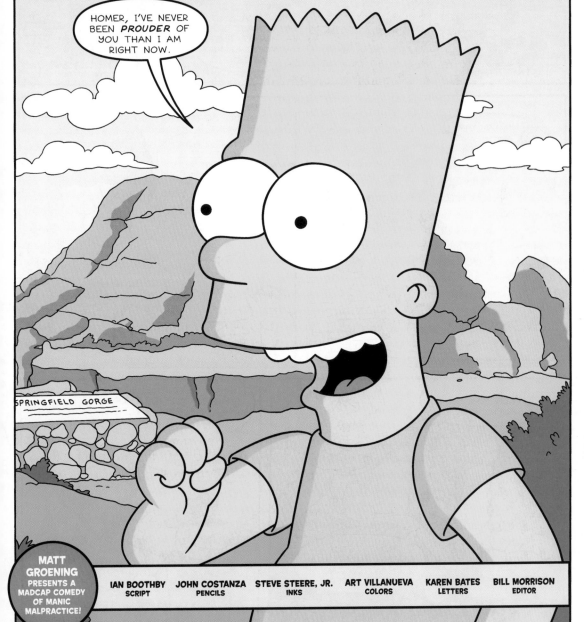

LAUGHTER is the WORST MEDICINE

HOMER, I'VE NEVER BEEN *PROUDER* OF YOU THAN I AM RIGHT NOW.

SPRINGFIELD GORGE

MATT GROENING PRESENTS A MADCAP COMEDY OF MANIC MALPRACTICE!

IAN BOOTHBY
SCRIPT

JOHN COSTANZA
PENCILS

STEVE STEERE, JR.
INKS

ART VILLANUEVA
COLORS

KAREN BATES
LETTERS

BILL MORRISON
EDITOR

DEAR LORD! AND I THOUGHT I SAW SOME *DISTURBING THINGS* IN 'NAM.

SHUCK!

CAN YOU *LEGALLY* USE THAT *ORIFICE?*

CHEW!

GULP! GULP!

GO, DAD, GO!

CAN'T ¡CHOMP!¿ LISTEN ¡MUNCH!¿ TO ENCOURAGEMENT! ¡GULP!¿ EATING!

MY SHUCKING FORK HAS *BROKEN!* THIS IS THE *GREATEST TRAGEDY* SINCE JOHN BYRNE'S "SPIDER MAN: CHAPTER ONE"!

AW, MAN! THIS *GUN HOLSTER* IS REALLY CUTTING INTO THE *OLD WAISTLINE.* COULD YOU HOLD IT FOR ME, CITIZEN?

YOU GOT IT, DUDE.

DAD, ALL YOU HAVE TO DO IS FINISH THAT ONE LAST HOT DOG, AND YOU'RE *THE CHAMP!*

DO IT, HOMER!

YES, DON'T LET OUR DEATHS BE IN VAIN!

¡GULP!¿

STUFF!

LADIES AND GENTLEMEN, WE HAVE A WINNER!

88

A LITTLE LATER AT SPRINGFIELD UNIVERSITY...

POW!

OOF!

SCREEEEE!

SPRINGFIELD UNIVERSITY

RAINIER WOLFCASTLE, FOR *OUTSTANDING ACTION ACTING* WE ARE PROUD TO PRESENT YOU WITH THIS *HONORARY DEGREE.* CONGRATULATIONS, *DOCTOR* WOLFCASTLE.

DIS IS DA *PROUDEST MOMENT* I'VE HAD ALL WEEK.

WHAM!

GAH!

OW!

AM I TOO LATE FOR MY *PHONY* DEGREE? I HAD A GIG I COULDN'T GET OUT OF!

YOU'RE NEXT AFTER THE DANCING BABY FROM "ALLY MCBEAL."

BACK OF THE LINE, BUB!

UH...DEAN PETERSON?

WHAT?

WE'VE *RUN OUT* OF THE HONORARY DOCTOR DECREES.

BUT...

WELL, GET *SOMETHING!* OR WE'LL REALLY HURT HIS FEELINGS.

NOW!

DIPLOMAS

AND SO FOR GIVING US THE MOST VALUABLE NON-MONETARY GIFT OF ALL, *THE GIFT OF LAUGHTER,* WE ARE HONORED TO PRESENT YOU WITH *THIS.*

THANKS. THIS IS WHAT MAKES ALL THE *SELTZER BURNS* AND *CUSTARD PIE-RELATED EYE INFECTIONS* WORTHWHILE!

AFTER THE CEREMONY...

SO WHAT DID WE END UP GIVING KRUSTY?

A *REAL* DOCTOR'S DEGREE.

PFFFFFFT!

SIR, I REPRESENT THE ESTATE OF THE LATE *DANNY THOMAS*. I HAVE A *COURT ORDER* DEMANDING YOU *DESIST* FROM PERFORMING HIS *COPYRIGHTED SPIT TAKE!*

MEANWHILE...

HOW'S DAD?

WELL, I HAVE SOME *GOOD NEWS* AND SOME *BAD NEWS*.

THE *GOOD NEWS* IS THE *DAMAGE* TO THE BRAIN WAS *ISOLATED* TO A VERY SMALL AREA.

THE BAD NEWS IS THAT IT SEEMS HOMER OVERLOADED *THE FOOD PLEASURE CENTER* OF HIS BRAIN.

WHICH MEANS?

I'LL NEVER ENJOY FOOD AGAIN.

⌐GASP!⌐

PAGING DR. HIBBERT, *CODE PUCE*.

I HAVE TO GO. SORRY.

THANK GOODNESS YOU'RE HERE, DOCTOR.

HI, DR. HIBBERT!

HI, DR. NICK!

THIS NURSE SAYS I CAN'T USE THESE *ELECTRO THINGIES* TO BRING THIS BOY'S GOLDFISH BACK TO LIFE.

I THINK I GAVE IT TOO MUCH GINGER ALE.

SHE'S RIGHT. I CAN'T ALLOW SUCH A *BLATANT MISUSE* OF HOSPITAL EQUIPMENT.

AW! BUT THEY'RE ALL *CHARGED UP* AND EVERY-THING.

I'LL GO AND FLUSH HIM LIKE DADDY DID WITH THE FERRET.

OOOPS!

TRIP!

ZAP!

IT SMELLS LIKE *KRUSTY BURGERS*!

HEY! MY FISH IS *ALIVE*! YAY!

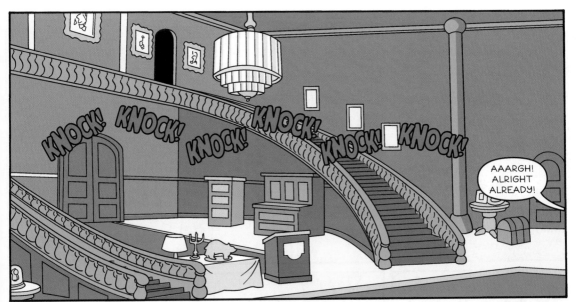

KNOCK! KNOCK! KNOCK! KNOCK! KNOCK! KNOCK!

AAARGH! ALRIGHT ALREADY!

IT'S EIGHT A.M.! IF THIS IS JOEY BISHOP, I'M NOT GONNA GIVE YOU LIZA'S NEW NUMBER! A *RESTRAINING ORDER* IS A RESTRAINING...

HELLO, MR. THE CLOWN. I HAVE SOMETHING IMPORTANT TO TELL YOU.

MOMENTS LATER...

HOLY SCHLAMOZZEL! SO I'M A REAL DOC?

THAT MEANS I CAN WRITE *MY OWN PRESCRIPTIONS,* RIGHT?

WELL, UM...YES, BUT FIRST...

YOU HAVE TO *TAKE CARE OF THEM!*

I THINK I DONE SPRAINED MY *COTTON PICKIN' BONE*.

I AIN'T LOOKING AFTER THESE SHLUBS. I KNOW *JACK* AND *SQUAT* ABOUT MEDICINE, AND JACK JUST LEFT TOWN!

WITH DR. HIBBERT AND DR. NICK OUT OF COMMISSION, YOU'RE THE *ONLY DOCTOR IN TOWN*, AND BY LAW YOU *HAVE TO* TAKE OVER FOR THEM.

OR WHAT?

LUNGE!

OH, CAN I ANSWER THAT?

TOWN CHARTER

YAAAH!

I'M REQUIRED BY *TOWN CHARTER* TO PLACE YOU ON THE RACK AND EXTEND YOUR ARMS AND LEGS 12 CUBITS. THEN THERE'S SOME STUFF ABOUT RATS AND HONEY.

MAN, THEY REALLY KNEW HOW TO MAKE *COOL LAWS* BACK IN THE *1600S*.

SO SHOULD I STRIP DOWN TO MY *SKIVVIES*, OR IS IT *THE FULL MONTY*?

:SIGH.:

AND SO...

AAAAAAAR!

GAH! NURSE TEENY, GET ME 30 CCS OF TIC TACS, *STAT*!

HEY, HOMER, YOU HAVEN'T TOUCHED YOUR BEER NUT MIX. MOE EVEN PUT IN SOME CEREAL HE WAS TOO SICK TO EAT THIS MORNING.

BEER MIX HAS JUST LOST ITS *MYSTERY* TO ME.

GEEZ, HOMER, IT'S WEIRD SEEIN' YA LIKE THIS. YOUR *CONSISTENT GLUTTONY* HAS ALWAYS BEEN...WHATAYACALL... COMFORTING.

I THINK I'LL JUST HEAD HOME AND GO TO BED EARLY.

IT'S *WORSE* THAN I THOUGHT.

AAAH! MARGE!

THANKS FOR LETTING ME *SPY* ON HIM MOE.

NO PROBLEM, MARGE.

AAAH! MOE!

SAY, MARGE, WHY DIDN'T YOU JUST PLAY CARL AND MOE PLAY MOE?

OH, THANKS A LOT, LENNY. NO, "WHAT *FANTASTIC MASKS* AND *IMPRESSIONS*, MOE AND MARGE!" JUST PICK, PICK, PICK!

MEANWHILE...

DOCTOR, IT HURTS WHEN I DO THIS.

DON'T DO THAT!

HA, HA!

HEY, THE LAUGHING MADE THE PAIN GO AWAY. THANKS, DR. KRUSTY.

DOCTOR, ALL THE DISAPPOINTMENT I HAVE IN SEYMOUR IS GIVING ME A *SPLITTING HEADACHE.*

I RECOMMEND PLENTY OF FLUIDS.

WHAT THE...? :SPUTTER:

SSSSTT!

HA, HA!

THAT CURED IT! YOU'RE A *MIRACLE WORKER!*

SAY, THIS GIG AIN'T AS HARD AS IT SEEMS.

NOW, KRUSTY, DON'T GET *OVER CONFIDENT!* THIS IS A *GREAT RESPONSIBILITY!*

YEAH, YEAH, YOU DON'T HAVE TO HIT ME OVER THE HEAD.

SPEAKING OF WHICH...

WHAM!

GAH!

HA!

HA!

HA!

HA!

SO IF THEY DON'T MAKE IT, YOU'LL **NEVER** GO BACK TO CLOWNING?

I GUESS NOT.

GET HIM OUT OF HERE! HE WAS TRYING TO **PULL THE PLUG** ON US.

IT LOOKED *FRAYED*. I WAS JUST CHECKING FOR *FAULTY WIRING*.

SO, NOW THAT YOU'RE A DOCTOR, WHO'S DOING YOUR SHOW?

⌐SHUDDER.⌐ SIDESHOW MEL.

AHEM. WHY DID THE VACUUM CLEANER CROSS THE ROAD?

BECAUSE IT SUCKED ALMOST AS BAD AS YOU!

MAN, I MISS THAT.

EVEN THE *HECKLING*?

PAGING DR. KRUSTY! THEY NEED YOU BACK AT YOUR HOME CLINIC. PAGING DR. KRUSTY.

⌐SIGH.⌐ YEAH.

THE END

WHY, HELLO, ALL MY FRIENDS IN *TELEVISION LAND!* WELCOME TO ANOTHER EPISODE OF *"DOWN-HOME DOCTORIN' TIME."* I'M YOUR HOST, DR. JULIUS HIBBERT.

AH HEE HEE HEE!

DAC-TAH, WHAD ABOUD MY *FADE?* MY *HODDIBLE, REPULDIVE FADE?*

SIMPLY *APPLY* A *GENEROUS COATING* OF THIS *OINTMENT* DIRECTLY TO THE FACIAL AREA *NINE TIMES A DAY*, AND YOU'LL BE *FIGHTIN' OFF THE LADIES* IN NO TIME!

LADIES? HOT *DOG!*

ZITROMEX

OH, I'M AFRAID YOUR *HOT DOG* DAYS ARE *OVER*, SON! THE *VOLATILE NATURE* OF THIS OINTMENT MAKES IT *DEADLY* FOR YOU TO INGEST MEAT PRODUCTS. IN FACT, *SOLID FOODS* ARE PRETTY MUCH BYE-BYE FOR THE *NEXT DECADE* OR SO.

HERE, HAVE A *LOLLY*. FOR A *SPECIAL TREAT* ONCE A DAY, YOU CAN *SMELL THE WRAPPER!*

SORRY ABOUT THAT, FOLKS! NEVER *SLOWS DOWN* HERE AT SPRINGFIELD HOSPITAL. YOU NEVER KNOW *WHAT* SORT OF *CRISIS* MIGHT CROP UP NEXT!

¡SNIFF!¡ ¡SNIFF!¡

DR. HIBBERT! COME *QUICKLY!* SOMEONE'S TOUCHING YOUR *NOVELTY GOLF-BALL-SHAPED COFFEE MUG!*

CANDICE

GOOD LORD, *NO!*

:SNIFF!:

AH HEE HEE HEE!

:SNIFF!:

DON'T *WORRY*, JULIUS. I KNOW YOU *ENJOYED* DOING YOUR TV SHOW, BUT *I STILL LOVE YOU!* WE'LL BE *FINE*.

:SNIFF: IN MY WHOLE LIFE I'VE ONLY HAD *TWO DREAMS*: TO BE A *TV DOCTOR* AND TO *ENDORSE* A *FROZEN PUDDING PRODUCT*.

RING! RING!

WHO ARE ALL THESE *CHILDREN*, BY THE WAY?

IT'S FOR YOU, JULIUS! IT'S THE *STUDIO!*

IT'S *OFFICIAL*, DOC! WE GOT *PICKED UP* BY *ANOTHER NETWORK!*

ALL WE HAVE TO DO IS MAKE A *FEW MINOR CHANGES!*

110

OH...MY. SO...GLAD...TO SEE YOU. WELCOME...TO SPRINGFIELD HOSPITAL, THE HOTTEST HOSPITAL IN THE STATE! OOOH!
CANDI

OOOOH... WHY NOT GET... COMFORTABLE?
THE DOCTOR WILL SEE YOU IN JUST A JOT... OOOOOH!
CANDI

BAD SKIN, BAD KNEES
WHAT'S YOUR DISEASE?
THE DOCTOR WILL PRESCRIBE SOME DRUGS
TO PUT YOU AT EASE!
WHEN DRUG-CRAZED ANIMALS
ATTACK NAUGHTY NURSES
IN HIGH-SPEED CHASES!
with your host
DR. JULIUS HIBBERT
BAD HEART, BAD BACK
WHEN THEY ALL ATTACK
HE'LL KICK DEATH IN THE KIDNEYS
WITH A MIGHTY WHACK!

SPRINGFIELD ELEMENTARY

RRRRRING!

"THERE'S THE BELL. *ENTER* OF YOUR OWN *FREE WILL!*"

"THAT'S IT. YOU'RE ALMOST THERE. IS THAT *FEAR* I SMELL? NO, WAIT! IT'S..."

SNIFF! SNIFF! "...*MINT?*"

"IS THAT *GUM?* DO YOU HAVE ENOUGH FOR *EVERYONE?*"

"I THOUGHT NOT. SPIT IT OUT AND TURN LEFT AT THE CAFETERIA."

TODAY'S SPECIAL: YESTERDAY'S SPECIAL

"*THIS* IS *IT.* NOW, HERE IS A *POP QUIZ.* REMEMBER TO SHOW ALL YOUR WORK IN THE MARGIN."

TEACHERS ONLY

"THE *QUESTION?* DO YOU DARE ENTER..?"

...THE PERMANENT RECORD ROOM!

IAN BOOTHBY
STORY

PHIL ORTIZ
PENCILS

ART VILLANUEVA
COLORS

SCOTT MCRAE, MIKE DECARLO, HOWARD SHUM
INKS

KAREN BATES
LETTERS

BILL MORRISON
EDITOR

MATT GROENING
ARCHIVIST

IS THAT A *SPIDER WEB*? THIS PLACE IS *FILTHY*! HONESTLY, WILLIE. WHAT DO WE PAY YOU FOR?

THEY PAY ME FOR NOT THROTTLING YOU, YA BUTTER TART BAKIN' FLOUR SIFTER.

WHAT WAS THAT, WILLIE?

I SAID I CANNAE WAIT TO HEAR YER STORIES.

VERY WELL THEN. OUR FIRST TALE, COINCIDENTALLY ENOUGH, STARTS WITH A SPIDER AND A GROUNDS-KEEPER.

"PRANKS, BUT NO PRANKS!"

"WE BEGIN IN A FILTHY SHACK ON THE EDGE OF THE SCHOOL GROUNDS."

ACH! WILLIE'LL NEVER HAVE ANOTHER *HAGGIS AND WHISKY SMOOTHIE NIGHTCAP* AGAIN.

I FEEL LIKE ALL OF *GLASGOW* IS HAVING A *FOOTBALL MATCH* IN ME *HEAD*.

ACH! A *SPIDER!*

WELL, GOTTA GET TA WORK. I'M SURE SOME KID'S *PUKE* NEEDS *SAW-DUSTING!*

BY SEAN CONNERY'S BACK HAIR!

WILLIE CAN WALK ON *CEILINGS!*

THAT SPIDER MUST HAVE *BIT ME* AND GIVEN ME *POWERS!*

ALL RIGHT, CLASS, TEACHER NEEDS SOME *QUIET TIME* IN THE TEACHER'S LOUNGE WITH HER LAWYER TO GO OVER *ALIMONY PAYMENTS*. SO *ASSISTANT GROUNDSKEEPER SEAMUS* IS GOING TO TELL YOU ALL ABOUT THE *HISTORY* OF *ST. PATRICK'S DAY*.

SURE'N YOU YOUNG ONES MUST BE WONDERIN' WHY I *PAINTED ME- SELF GREEN* T'DAY. WELL, T'WAS YOUNG BART'S IDEA, AND...

YAAAA!

ACH! THIS SWINGIN'S HARDER THAN IT LOOKS!

SMASH!

DINNA WORRY, WEE BAIRNS. IT'S ONLY YOUR *FRIENDLY NEIGHBORHOOD WILLIE WEBSPINNER*.

SEYMOUR!

I'M BUSY, MOTHER!

WHAT ARE YOU DOING IN HERE?

NARRATING, MOTHER.

THAT BETTER NOT MEAN WHAT I *THINK* IT DOES!

≋SIGH≋ OUR NEXT FABLE STARTS WITH A BOY AND *HIS* MOTHER. IT WAS ONE YEAR AGO...

"AND THE BEATINGS GO ON!"

I'M *NERVOUS*, MOM. A *NEW SCHOOL*. WHAT IF THE KIDS DON'T *LIKE* ME?

DON'T WORRY, JAMES. JUST MAKE A GOOD *FIRST IMPRESSION*, AND YOU'LL MAKE LOTS OF NEW FRIENDS. AND ALWAYS REMEMBER...

SOON...

MENU

SORRY, YOU CAN'T ENTER THE LUNCHROOM WITHOUT ANSWERING A SIMPLE QUESTION.

⋛SIGH⋚ WHAT IS IT?

WHO WAS THE *FIRST* CAPTAIN OF THE U.S.S. ENTERPRISE?

I DON'T KNOW. LUKE SKYWALKER?

HA! HA! HA! HA!

WHAT A JIMBO!

IT'S NOT FAIR!

FORGET IT, JIMBO. THIS IS *NERDTOWN*.

FOR AS LONG AS ANYONE CAN REMEMBER, *NERDS* HAVE *RULED* THIS SCHOOL WITH A MIX OF *HIGH G.P.A.S*, *PERFECT ATTENDANCE*, AND *CRUELTY*.

HEY, JIMBO, THINK AT 299,792,458 METERS PER SECOND!

WHAT?

SPLOOOSH!

SNAP!

HA! HA! HA! HA! HA! HA! HA!

UGH!

GAK!

AAARG!

THAT WAS SO...

EMPOWERING!

AND ALL THIS *MONEY* FELL OUT OF THEIR POCKETS WHEN WE WERE BEATING ON THEM.

GOOD JOB, GUYS!

FINALLY OUR SCHOOL IS *FREE FROM BULLIES!*

WHERE DO YOU THINK *YOU'RE* GOING?

HOME.

YOU DIDN'T PAY "THE LEAVING SCHOOL WITHOUT A FAT LIP" TAX.

:GULP: BUT I DON'T HAVE ANY MONEY.

HEY, WANNA EAT SOMETHING? I'M STARVED.

YEAH, BUT WHAT DO YOU WANNA DO WITH THE REST OF THE MONEY?

LET'S *INVEST* IN *DOT COMS*. THEIR STOCK JUST KEEPS GROWING LIKE A BUBBLE THAT CAN NEVER BURST.

YES, IN THE END THE *NERDS* HAD THE *LAST LAUGH. IRONIC,* DON'T YOU THINK?

SKINNER!

SUPERINTENDENT CHALMERS!

THAT WAS THE WORST NON-ALANIS MORRISETTE-RELATED EXAMPLE OF IRONY I'VE EVER HEARD!

THE BULLIES GOT THEIR MONEY FROM NERDS, THEN INVESTED IT IN NERD-RUN DOT COMS AND LOST EVERYTHING.

O. HENRY, YOU ARE NOT.

OH, AND *YOU* COULD TELL A BETTER STORY?

YES, AND MINE WILL HAVE A *GREAT* TWIST ENDING!

WE'LL START THIS TALE A LONG TIME AGO IN A SCHOOL DISTRICT NOT TOO FAR AWAY.

CAN I HAVE MORE SYRUP FOR MY WAFFLES?

SYRUP'S FOR SISSIES! I WON'T HAVE IT IN MY HOUSE! *UNSWEETENED MOLASSES!* THAT'S GOOD ENOUGH!

NOW, ABE...

"TRUANT OR FALSE?"

"AND SO HOMER *DID* GO TO SCHOOL AND *STUDIED HARD.*"

"BUT SCHOOL WAS *BORING,* HE *LOST INTEREST* IN A FEW MINUTES, AND GREW UP TO BE *FAT, DUMB* AND *BALD.*"

"AND WHAT OF THE *YOUNG REBEL BOY* WHO LOST HIS *ONLY FRIEND* THAT DAY?"

"HOMER'S WORDS ABOUT EDUCATION SAT IN THE BACK OF HIS MIND FOR YEARS, AND THAT *YOUNG HELLION* GREW UP TO BE..."

"...KING OF THE VAMPIRES!"

HE DID NOT! HE GREW UP TO BE *ME*! *PRINCIPAL* SEYMOUR SKINNER!

YES, BUT YOU'RE *BORING*. I'VE ALWAYS LIKED STORIES THAT ENDED WITH VAMPIRES BEST.

BUT THAT'S NOT THE POINT! THESE WERE *MORALITY TALES* THAT...

ARE YE DONE IN HERE?

YES, WE ARE, WILLIE. IT'S ALL YOURS.

LOOK, I EVEN FOUND SOME COOL VAMPIRE TEETH IN THAT BOX OVER THERE.

THAT'S THE *CONFISCATION BIN*. THOSE WERE IN *RALPH WIGGUM'S* MOUTH.

GOOD LORD! ‡CHOKE!‡

NOW THAT THEY'RE FINISHED WI' THEIR SISSY STORIES...

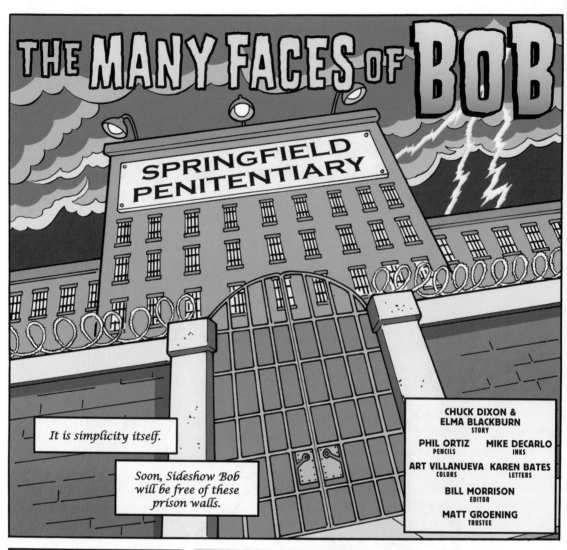

THE MANY FACES OF BOB

SPRINGFIELD PENITENTIARY

It is simplicity itself.

Soon, Sideshow Bob will be free of these prison walls.

CHUCK DIXON &
ELMA BLACKBURN
STORY

PHIL ORTIZ
PENCILS

MIKE DECARLO
INKS

ART VILLANUEVA
COLORS

KAREN BATES
LETTERS

BILL MORRISON
EDITOR

MATT GROENING
TRUSTEE

An odiferous, but mercifully brief, sojourn through the soil pipe beneath Cell Block Seven.

I emerge in the steamy confines of the prison laundry.

Then slip unnoticed over the evening step aerobics class.

I remove my cache of purloined leotards from the locker room.

Hastily, but surely, I sew the colorful garments together...

...seal the freshly-joined seams with rubber cement cadged over time from my photo-collage class...

RUBBER CEMENT

...inflate my ingeniously designed vehicle over the vents of the sauna in Block Ten.

...then float from this wretched place on a light zephyr of wind, launching from off the handball courts.

And thus I take the first step toward my ultimate goal...

...THE DEATH OF BART SIMPSON.

SIDESHOW BOB!

THAT NIGHT...

WE'LL SEARCH SPRINGFIELD'S BACK ALLEYS AND LONELY STREETS UNTIL WE *FIND* SIDESHOW BOB AND UNMASK HIM.

UH... OKAY.

HOURS LATER...

WE SPIED IN EVERY WINDOW IN TOWN AND LEARNED *NOTHING*.

EXCEPT THAT YOUR AUNT SELMA'S *ELECTROLYSIS* ISN'T TAKING. 'EW!'

I'LL *FIND* YOU, SIDESHOW BOB!

AND WHEN I DO, YOU'LL KNOW THE *WRATH OF BARTMAN!*

HA! HA! HA! HA! HA! HA! HA! HA! HA! HA!

THAT CREEPY LAUGHTER!

THE CHUCKLING OF A DEMON SPAWNED *MADMAN!*

WHAT'S SO *FUNNY*, DADDY?

HO-HEH. THAT SLUGGO...WHAT A *SCAMP*.

IT'S *HOPELESS*. I'LL *NEVER* FIND SIDESHOW BOB. I SHOULD JUST LAY HERE UNTIL HE *KILLS* ME.

GAAAAAAAAH!

SORRY IF I *WOKE* YOU, SWEETIE. I COULDN'T SLEEP SO I THOUGHT I'D DO SOME *LATE NIGHT DUSTING*.

:PANT: :PANT: :PANT: :PANT:

WHAT'S THE *MATTER*, SON? YOU'RE NOT EATING YOUR CEREAL.

WHY GO ON EATING WHEN, AT ANY MOMENT, MY TOO-SHORT LIFE WILL *END* AT THE HANDS OF A MANIAC CLOWN?

NO SENSE IN WASTING THIS. *YOINK!*

I MAY HAVE *SOLVED* YOUR PROBLEM, BART.

YOU MEAN A WAY TO *REMOVE* THE DEATH SENTENCE HANGING OVER ME?

NO, BUT I HAVE A LIST OF PEOPLE WHO *COULD* BE SIDESHOW BOB *IN DISGUISE*.

MYUM! MYUSH! SMACK!

ELEMENTARY SCHOOL WELCOMES NEW SUBSTITUTE TEACHER.

Howard Stamper looks forward to teaching eager youngsters when regular teachers call in sick.

SOCIETY PAGE

Vanetta Wellbourne, heir to the Wellbourne Foot Powder fortune, visits Springfield to judge flower show.

NEWS OF THE HOMELESS

Call me a hobo. Known only as "Stinky", this new visitor will be gracing the homeless shelters and public libraries of our town after two years of living under the train station in Ogdenville. "Stinky" enjoys walks in the rain, people who are "real," and the dumpster behind the Kwik-e-Mart.

NONE OF THESE LOSERS LOOK LIKE SIDESHOW BOB.

THAT'S THE *POINT.* WITH A NEW FACE AND BOB'S ABILITIES AS A *THESPIAN,* HE COULD BE *ANY* OF THESE *NEWCOMERS.*

COULD BE...

IT'S *DECIDED,* THEN. WE BEGIN *INTENSE,* AROUND-THE-CLOCK-SURVEILLANCE. AS SOON AS *SCHOOL* LETS OUT.

AS I *SUSPECTED!* YOU'RE NO HOMELESS *WRETCH!*

HUH?

I *KNOW* WHO YOU ARE!

NO!

YOU CAN'T HIDE FROM *ME.* YOUR *SHAME* FOLLOWS *WHEREVER* YOU GO!

CAN I *NEVER* ESCAPE MY PAST?

I CREATED *NEW* COKE! IT WAS *ME!* I HAD THE *HUBRIS* TO TAMPER WITH THE WORLD'S MOST POPULAR SOFT DRINK AND *PAID* THE PRICE!

OH MY *GOSH*, BART. WE'VE FORCED A MAN TO RE-VISIT THE WORST MOMENTS OF HIS LIFE. WHAT A *HORRIBLE* MISTAKE.

YEAH. THREE HOURS IN MAKE-UP DOWN THE TUBES.

WHY? WHY DID I TRY AND PLAY *GOD?*

ON TO SUSPECT TWO.

El Barto

152

RING! RING!

HELLO?

IS THIS MRS. EDNA KRABAPPEL?

YES.

I HAVE SOME *BAD* NEWS FOR YOU. YOUR UNCLE FLETCHER HAS PASSED ON.

I DON'T REMEMBER *HAVING* AN UNCLE FLETCHER.

WELL, HE REMEMBERED *YOU* TO THE TUNE OF *ONE MILLION DOLLARS!*

BUT YOU ONLY HAVE *ONE HOUR* TO GET TO THE READING OF HIS WILL AT THE NORTH HAVERBROOK COURTHOUSE.

WHA--?

MRS. KRABAPPEL? HELLO?

BRING ON THE *SUBSTITUTE TEACHER.*

NOW OPEN YOUR SOCIAL STUDIES BOOKS TO PAGE FORTY ONE.

CLASS...

MR. Stamper

FIND OUT WHAT THE MUSIC IS, BART.

WHAT GOOD IS *THAT* GOING TO DO?

WHAT WOULD *BOB* LISTEN TO? IF IT'S ANYTHING FROM HEAVY CLASSICAL TO LIGHT OPERA THEN THE SUB *COULD* BE OUR MAN.

GOTCHA, SIS!

GLUE

EWWWWW...

ENYA.

{ICK!} NO *WAY* THAT'S BOB.

QUITE THE LITTLE *NANCY DREW*, AREN'T WE? I *KNEW*, IF I BIDED MY TIME, YOUR *CURIOSITY* WOULD EVENTUALLY BRING YOU HERE.

AND NOW YOU WILL MEET THE *HIDEOUS FATE* YOU HAVE SO LONG *AVERTED*.

BUT I THOUGHT YOU HAD YOUR *FACE* CHANGED. YOU STILL LOOK THE *SAME*.

DON'T BE *RIDICULOUS*, BOY.

WITH THE EYE-TUCK, THE DERMA-BRASION AND FRUIT ACID PEEL, I LOOK *YEARS* YOUNGER.

BUT IF FOR THAT INSULT *ALONE*, I WILL NOW END YOUR SHORT AND MEDDLE-SOME EXISTENCE.

GAAAAAAH!

BONK!

UH!

SIDESHOW MEL?

I COULD NOT STAND BY AND **ALLOW** MY PREDECESSOR TO GIVE VENT TO HIS HOMICIDAL URGES ONCE MORE.

SO WHY DIDN'T YOU BUST HIM **BEFORE** NOW?

I WANTED TO CAPTURE HIM IN THE ACT. AND I WASN'T CERTAIN IT **WAS** HIM. BOB'S GIFTS AS A METHOD ACTOR ARE UNEQUALED.

YOU SAVED MY **LIFE**.

YOU'RE A **PART** OF KRUSTY'S **SHRINKING** VIEWERSHIP. CALL IT **SELF-PRESERVATION**.

WHAT HAPPENS TO BOB **NOW**?

HE RETURNS TO INCARCERATION TO BE LOCKED **AWAY** FROM THE REST OF THE WORLD WITH ALL THE **OTHER** MISCREANTS AND SOCIOPATHS.

URRRRRMMMM...

I JUST WANT TO MAKE **SURE** MY WIFE TAPED THE GAME!

YOU'RE NOT USING **MY** MINUTES!

IT'S THE **SERIES**, MAN!

MY RATES GO **DOWN** AT **NINE**.

THE **GAME** STARTS AT **SEVEN**!

THE END

HOMER VS. THE RACCOON

TONY DIGEROLAMO	BRIAN ILES	MIKE ROTE	CHRIS UNGAR	KAREN BATES	BILL MORRISON	MATT GROENING
SCRIPT	PENCILS	INKS	COLORS	LETTERS	EDITOR	PEST CONTROLLER

162

THE NEXT DAY...

DADDY'S NOT A MONSTER. I'M GOING TO CRUSH THE RACCOON'S *SKULL* THE *HUMANE* WAY.

DAD, YOU CAN'T KILL THE RACCOON! IT'S *INHUMANE*!

HI-DIDDLY-HO, NEIGHBORINO!

NNNGUH! GAAAHH!

CAN'T HELP BUT NOTICE YOU'VE GOT AN *ANVIL* SUSPENDED OVER MY NEW TRASHCANS.

YOU CAN'T EXPECT ME TO USE *MY* TRASH-CANS. YOUR TRASHCANS ARE THE *THING*--YOU KNOW, LIKE IN AN *EXPERIMENT*.

YOU MEAN "*THE CONTROL ELEMENT*"?

YES! THANK YOU. THAT'S WHY I CAN'T DESTROY *MY* TRASHCANS.

I DON'T KNOW ABOUT THIS. WOULDN'T *MAGGIE* BE BETTER FOR THIS TRAP? SHE'S THE *SIZE* OF A RACCOON.

THERE IT GOES, HOMER!

SMASH!

YOINK!

HOMER vs. THE RACCOON II

SCREECH!

YOU PUT THE *RECYCLABLES* ON THE *ROOF?*

WELL, YOU CAN'T *MIX* PAPER AND PLASTIC, MARGE! YOU *CAN'T!*

LATER...

WE CAN'T *LIVE* LIKE THIS.

WELL, IF YOU HAVE A *BETTER WAY* TO KEEP THE RACCOON OUT OF OUR TRASH, *I'D* LIKE TO *HEAR* IT.

I'LL HELP YOU, DAD, BUT ONLY IF YOU *PROMISE* TO USE *HUMANE METHODS.*

HUMANE? OH. ARE *CLUBS* CONSIDERED HUMANE?

NO!

ALL RIGHT, WE'LL TRY IT *YOUR* WAY.